LEGO NINJAGO

BRICK ADVENTURES
3 NEW ACTION-PACKED, ILLUSTRATED STORIES!

SCHOOL FOR CROOKS

By Meredith Rusu

SCHOLASTIC INC.

Published by Scholastic Inc., *Publishers since 1920*. SCHOLASTIC and associated logos are trademarks and/or registered trademarks of Scholastic Inc.

The publisher does not have any control over and does not assume any responsibility for author or third-party websites or their content.

This book is a work of fiction. Names, characters, places, and incidents are either the product of the author's imagination or are used fictitiously, and any resemblance to actual persons, living or dead, business establishments, events, or locales is entirely coincidental.

ISBN 978-1-338-26249-0

10 9 8 7 6 5 4 3 2 1   18 19 20 21 22

Printed in the U.S.A.   40
First printing 2018

CONTENTS

PEOPLE YOU WILL MEET

LLOYD:
The Green Ninja

KAI:
Ninja and Master of Fire

NYA:
Ninja and Master of Water

JAY:
Ninja and Master of
Lightning

ZANE:
Ninja and Master of Ice. Also
known as the Titanium Ninja

COLE:
Ninja and Master of Earth

MASTER WU:
The ninja's teacher

SKYLOR:
Ninja and Master of Amber

RONIN:
A friend of the ninja

PRINCESS HARUMI:
Daughter of Ninjago's emperor
and empress

FROM THE JOURNAL OF LLOYD, THE GREEN NINJA

THINGS FEEL DIFFERENT WITH THE NINJA these days. Ever since we lost **Master Wu**, our team has been a bit lost, too.

A year has passed since Master Wu disappeared. We don't know where he is. But we are determined to bring him home.

So our team has split up. **Kai** and **Zane** are tracking down leads. **Nya** has gone north to search for clues. And **Jay** and **Cole** have traveled to a mountain **monastery**, where an old man with no memory is living among the monks. They hope he might be our missing master.

Meanwhile, I'm keeping watch at home. There is new threat here. A mysterious biker gang called the **Sons of Garmadon** is searching for three legendary **Oni Masks**.

Anyone who finds all three masks will become all-powerful.

The gang has already stolen one mask from **Borg Industries**. The second mask is safe at the Royal Family's palace. No one knows how to find the third mask.

Ninjago's emperor and empress have asked us to protect them and their daughter, **Princess Harumi**. So I must summon the team. Together, we will fight these new enemies.

But still, I am worried. Why is this biker gang after the Oni Masks? And why are they using my father's name?

Ever since the day I saw my father's face on the biker gang's logo, I can't shake the feeling that things are . . . different. Where is Master Wu? In this time of trouble, we need him now more than ever.

STORY #1:

SCHOOL FOR CROOKS

One month ago . . .

"A gang of criminals, you say?" Kai spoke into his **communicator**.

"Indeed," replied Zane from the other end. "The police commissioner has learned of a new crime ring recruiting members in Ninjago."

It was late afternoon. Kai and Zane had been trying to find their lost leader, Master Wu. Kai was feeling burned out, and that was saying something for the Master of Fire. So he headed to Master Chen's Noodle House for a spicy snack.

Kai was waiting for his food when he got Zane's message.

"Do the police know who the gang is?" Kai asked.

"Negative," Zane replied. "I will head to Borg Industries and search the internet for leads. We can meet once I have learned more."

"Sounds good," Kai said. He smiled as a young woman with red hair approached. She was holding a bowl of fresh noodles. "Over and out."

"Trouble?" the woman asked. Her eyes were sharp, but her smile was friendly.

It was **Skylor**, a good friend of Kai's. She used to be an **Elemental Master** like the ninja. She'd even competed in Master Chen's Tournament of Elements. Back then, she was one of the bad guys. But she'd left behind the criminal life. Now she ran the best noodle shop in town.

"Seems like there's always trouble in Ninjago City," Kai said. He took a big bite of noodles. "A new gang is recruiting members."

Skylor looked thoughtful. "I may know who you're talking about."

"Really?" Kai asked, surprised.

Skylor nodded. "Some guys from the docks were in here the other day. Things got . . . *interesting* when they couldn't pay their bill. So I taught them a lesson."

"You fought them?" Kai asked.

Skylor laughed. "Not exactly. I made them wash dishes. But while they were scrubbing pots and pans, one mentioned a new gang. It was called the School for Crooks."

"The School for Crooks," Kai repeated. "Thanks, Skylor. Zane and I will look into it."

"Hold on, hotshot," Skylor said. "How about the two of us follow this lead together, for old times' sake?"

"Just the two of us?" Kai asked.

Skylor shrugged. "Why not? We used to make a good team."

Kai thought for a moment. "I guess it would save time. But the last time we fought together, you were part of the gang."

Skylor grinned. "That makes me the perfect partner for this job, don't you think?"

That night, Kai and Skylor crept up to the darkest pier at the Ninjago City docks.

"Tell me again how you know about this place?" Kai asked.

"When you're Master Chen's daughter, you learn a thing or two," Skylor said. She scanned the shadowy docks. "There! Those are the guys from the other day."

She pointed to two workers with beards. They were talking with a man wearing a large hat. A dark mask covered the lower half of his face.

LET'S GO!

"Bet you a bowl of spicy noodles that's not the dock master," Kai said.

Slowly, Skylor and Kai sneaked up to them.

Suddenly, the man with the mask looked up. When he saw Kai and Skylor, he ran!

"Let's go!" Kai exclaimed.

He and Skylor raced after the masked figure, following him to the end of the dock. For a second, Kai thought the chase was over. But then the masked man took a giant leap . . . toward the water!

Kai and Skylor ran to the edge of the dock and looked over the side. The man had landed on a pillar poking up from the water. He was hopping across the pillars next to it, heading toward the next dock.

In a flash, Skylor and Kai hopped down to the pillar and matched the masked man's moves. They cornered him on the next dock.

"There's nowhere to run!" Kai shouted. "Unless you can run on water!"

The masked man glared at them. Then he flipped a lever hidden under his cloak. A jetpack on his back fired up, pushing him out and over the water!

"Aw, man, I was kidding!" Kai shouted.

"Better save the jokes for Jay," Skylor said. "Any ideas?"

"You know it," Kai said. "Time for a trick you've never seen. Grab on!"

Skylor grabbed Kai's back. He lifted his arms in the air, and a bright red glow surrounded them. A moment later, Kai used **Airjitzu** to fly them over the water!

"Looks like you ninja have been busy," Skylor said, impressed.

Kai grinned. "Looks like I can still surprise you."

"Looks like you should — LOOK OUT!" Skylor cried.

Kai had nearly spun them right into a cruise ship!

At the last second, Kai stopped. He and Skylor crashed down into a crowded dining area on the ship's deck.

"Is that how you always land?" Skylor asked, pulling salad out of her hair.

"Not exactly," Kai said. He hurried through tables. "Excuse me — sorry about that — mmmm, those noodles look tasty — pardon me."

Meanwhile, Skylor raced to the ship's railing. "There he is!" She pointed to the masked man. He was still powering along the water with his jetpack.

Suddenly, the masked man's jets sputtered. His fuel had run out! He dipped low over the water. Then he tumbled onto a pier.

"Now we've got him!" Skylor shouted. "Come on, Kai!"

TAKE THE WHEEL!

She leaped over the railing and onto a speedboat below. Kai jumped on board, and they zipped through the water, cutting a path straight toward the dock.

The masked man growled when he saw they were still chasing him.

"Take the wheel!" Skylor shouted to Kai.

Without warning, Skylor leaped from the speedboat up onto the dock!

"What about me?" Kai shouted after her.

"Find somewhere to dock!" Skylor shouted back. "Without crashing this time!" Then she dashed after the man.

The masked man picked up speed and leaped over a fence into the cargo area.

Skylor did the same.

He jumped over a dumpster and turned into an alleyway.

Skylor did, too.

Then he sped straight toward the brick walls lining the alley. He climbed up the walls to the rooftops!

"Oof." Skylor stretched her muscles. "It's been a while. Let's see if I've still got it."

With a deep breath, she ran straight toward the wall. Then she matched the masked man's moves, leaping up between the buildings. At last, she reached the rooftops.

"Give it up!" she yelled, cornering the masked man. "There's nowhere left to run."

The man turned to face her. Skylor was right — there was no way down without going past her. He tried to ignite his jetpack, but it was no use. He was out of fuel and out of escape routes.

Just then, Kai used Airjitzu to fly up beside her. He powered up a fireball.

"We can do this the easy way, or the hard way," Kai said.

The man peered at them for a moment. Then he removed his mask. "How about the 'old friends' way?"

"**Ronin**?!" Kai exclaimed.

Ronin was Ninjago's best bounty hunter. He was also the ninja's friend . . . most of the time.

"Heh." Ronin laughed. "Yeah, it's me. You two give quite the chase."

"I don't believe it," Kai said. "*You're* the one running the School for Crooks? But why?"

"I've got my reasons," Ronin replied. "The bigger question is, why are you two chasing me?"

"Because you're running a school for crooks!" Kai exclaimed.

YEAH, IT'S ME, RONIN.

"I didn't think crime gangs were your style," Skylor added.

Now Ronin frowned. "Crime gangs? What exactly do you think the School for Crooks is?"

Kai and Skylor exchanged a glance. "Uh . . . a school for crooks?" Kai said.

"Exactly." Ronin nodded. "A school to *reform* crooks. Help them get back on their feet and make new lives for themselves. Something we both know about." He gave Skylor a look.

"I'm very confused." Kai scratched his head. "If your school is to reform crooks, then why did the police commissioner tell Zane there's a new gang recruiting members?"

"Ohhh, *that*." Ronin chuckled. "Heh. That's not my group. But it's part of the reason my School for Crooks is up and running. The police chief wants to get ahead of that new gang's shady business. So we struck a deal. I get criminals off the street and back on their feet. And the police overlook some of my past, uh, activities. Win-win."

"Ahh," Skylor said. "Now, that *does* sound like your style."

"But if you're helping reform bad guys, then why did you run from us?" Kai asked.

"Being friends with the ninja isn't great for my reputation," Ronin said. "I get more students if it seems like I'm one of the crooks, you know? And I have to admit, it's fun seeing you chase me. Just like old times. Heh."

"He has a point," Skylor said to Kai. "Guess our lead turned out to be all wrong."

"Yeah, looks like it," Kai said. "Sorry we chased you, Ronin. Let us know if you need any help with your, uh, school."

"Sure thing." Ronin started to walk away. "I could always use help . . . with lunch duty. Working for the good guys gives me a big appetite. And Master Chen's **Puffy Potstickers** are the best."

STORY #2:

FORCED ENTRY

Far up north, a winding road snaked through rice fields. It stretched for miles. At the end was a village.

This wasn't an ordinary village. It was surrounded by a huge stone wall, twenty feet high and nearly as thick. A tall gate marked the entrance. A lone traveler slowly approached it.

The traveler stopped. She looked up. Her face was covered by a dark mask.

This was Nya, the Master of Water.

"No sign of Master Wu up north," she spoke into her communicator. "But I've found something else I need to take care of."

SOMEONE NEEDS TO LEARN A LESSON.

"Something serious?" asked Lloyd.

"Let's just say someone needs to learn a lesson," Nya answered.

Ever since Master Wu had disappeared, the ninja had been searching for their teacher. Nya's quest had brought her up north. She wasn't any closer to finding Master Wu. But she had heard rumors of a walled village ruled by a cruel master. People there worked long, hard hours for no money. And they weren't allowed to leave.

It was as unfair as unfair could get. And if there was one thing Nya wouldn't stand for, it was anything unfair.

As Nya approached the enormous gate, a guard stopped her.

"What are you doing here?" he demanded.

"I've come to visit the Master," Nya said.

The guard frowned. "The Master doesn't take visitors."

"This isn't a social call," Nya said. "It's more of a wake-up call."

The guard's frown grew deeper. "The Master is already awake," he said, confused. "And he doesn't take visitors. There is one rule here. No one in, no one out."

"Is that so?" Nya asked. She looked the guard up and down. He was big, sure. But not big enough to stop a *ninja*.

"Well, if that's the rule," Nya said, "then we'll have to keep things even. One in —"

Quick as a flash, Nya darted past the guard . . .

"— and one out!"

. . . she pushed him out through the gate!

"Whoa!" the guard cried, dizzy.

"Problem solved!" Nya said. She turned to make her way into the village.

Suddenly, a long shadow loomed over her.

"Is there a problem here?" a loud voice boomed.

A second guard stomped up. He was double the size of the first.

"Okay," Nya said. "Problem not solved."

"No one in, no one out," the guard grunted.

"Come on, guys," Nya said. "I'm sure you can make room for little old me."

She ran straight toward the guard, bounced off his leg, and flipped up and over his shoulder!

Nya was about to land when —

WHA-BOOM!

The guard knocked her back with one punch of his huge hand. Nya went flying through the gate. She skidded to a stop just outside the wall.

Nya looked up, more determined than before. "I didn't want to have to do this," she said. "But it looks like we're going to have to fight."

The guards laughed. "You will fight us? A little girl?"

Nya powered up a spinning ball of water. "I prefer *Master of Water*."

Suddenly, the two guards stopped laughing.

"The Master of Water?" the first whispered. "I've heard stories about her. She's a *ninja*."

"Yeah," the second guard said. "I heard she defeated the **Preeminent** with a single wave."

"I heard she destroyed the entire **Cursed Realm** — for *fun*."

Nya sighed. That last part wasn't exactly true. But it was better for them to think it was. "That's me," she said. "And I'd like to come in now."

The guards looked nervous, but they stood their ground. "No one in, no one out," they insisted.

"Suit yourself." Nya made her ball of water even larger. "*Ninja-GO!*"

She shot the huge burst straight at the guards! They braced for impact. Then —

Spritz.

The water fizzled out as soon as it crossed the gate.

"Huh," one said. "I thought that attack would be . . . wetter."

"What happened?" Nya asked. "It's like my water power was blocked by . . ." she trailed off, looking up at the gate.

Oh, no, she thought. *That gate must be made of* **vengestone**. *My elemental power won't work near it!*

NINJA-GO!

Meanwhile, the guards were laughing at her.

"The Master of Water isn't all she's hyped up to be," one said.

"Yeah." The other grinned. "Time for her to hit the road."

A few seconds later, Nya went sailing back down the long, winding path. She landed in a cloud of dirt.

"We told you!" The guards chuckled. "No one in, no one out." They slammed the gate shut.

Nya gritted her teeth. "That didn't go as planned. How am I going to get in? If I can't force my way in, I'll have to sneak past them somehow." Then Nya had an idea. "Could it be as simple as *following the rules*?"

Half an hour later, Nya approached the gate again. This time, she wasn't dressed in her gi. Instead, a plain scarf covered her face and a large rice hat sat on her head. She carried two

buckets of water on her back.

"What do you want?" the guards demanded.

"I'm from the village," Nya said meekly. "I went out for water."

"You WHAT?" the guards bellowed. "You know the Master's rule. No one in, no one out!"

"Oh, dear!" Nya said. "Will you be in trouble for letting me out?"

"Will *we* be in trouble?" one of the guards asked. Then he turned to the other. "Hey, will we?"

"Maybe," the larger guard said. "If she got out on our watch."

"Will the Master punish you?" Nya asked.

The guards gulped. "He might," one whispered to the other.

"I suppose I should go back in," Nya said. "So it's like I never got out."

"Yeah, yeah, that's a good idea," the guards said. "You were never out. Let's go with that. Get back to your field — now!"

"Oh, thank you." Nya quickly slipped past. "Thank you so much."

"Just keep quiet," the guards told her. "And stick to your work!"

Nya nodded. A smile crossed her face as she walked toward the Master's home. "I will," she said. "I've got my work cut out for me."

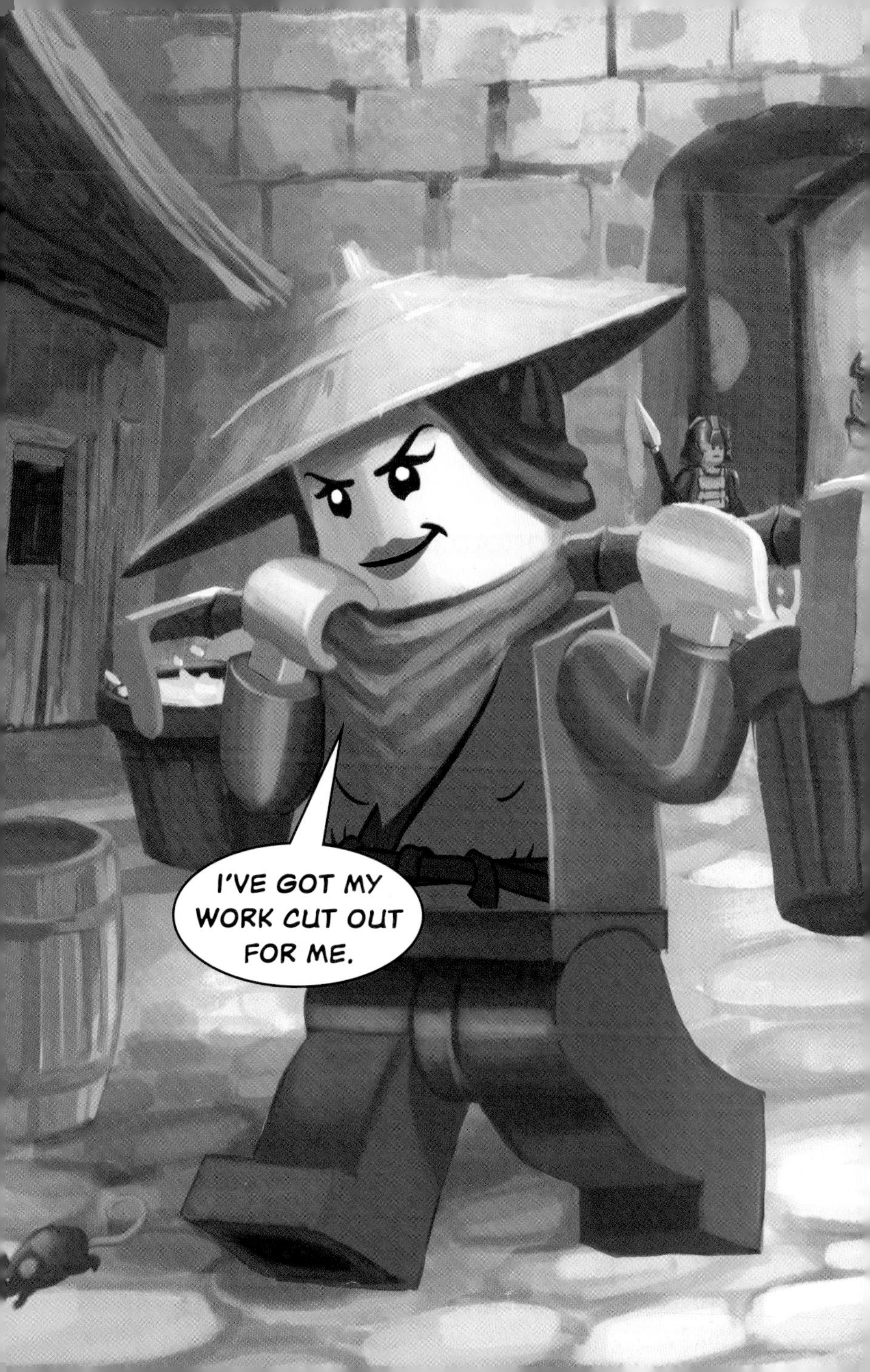
I'VE GOT MY WORK CUT OUT FOR ME.

STORY #3:

GETAWAY

High on a rooftop, **Lloyd** faced off against an unknown enemy. He and the other ninja were protecting the Royal Palace and the legendary Oni Masks from thieves. But while Lloyd was on patrol, someone had **ransacked** Princess Harumi's room.

The intruder was racing away. The mysterious thief was holding a sack large enough to fit a person. The princess must be inside!

"Who are you?" Lloyd demanded.

Without a word, the intruder removed her cloak, revealing it was —

Princess Harumi herself!

"Princess?" Lloyd exclaimed. "I thought you were being kidnapped! But if you're the intruder, then who's in the bag?"

"You mean *what's* in the bag," Princess Harumi said. She opened it, revealing piles of sandwiches, fruit, and water.

"Food for the needy," she explained. "Even though I have to stay inside the palace, I still try to give what I can."

"But your bedroom . . . it was ransacked," Lloyd insisted.

The princess blushed. "Yes, I can be very messy. *Thank you for noticing.*"

Now Lloyd blushed. He hadn't meant to insult the princess. In fact, he'd grown to like her. "I'm sorry," he started. "I didn't mean —"

Suddenly, Lloyd was interrupted by the sound of guards approaching.

"They can't know I'm away from the palace," Princess Harumi whispered. "Hurry, put these on." She snatched some old clothes from a nearby laundry line.

Lloyd draped the rags over his brightly colored gi. Then he and the princess slid down a long pipe to the street below.

But as their feet touched the ground, Lloyd and the princess froze. There were more guards marching nearby. Quickly, Lloyd and Princess Harumi hid behind more laundry.

"Question everyone," the leader told his troops. "Emperor and Empress's orders."

Princess Harumi gasped. "If they speak to us, they will realize who I am." She sounded nervous. "My parents will be furious if they discover what I've been doing."

Lloyd could see the worried look on Princess Harumi's face. He felt bad for her. The princess was only trying to help people in need. She shouldn't get into trouble for that.

"Don't worry, Princess," he said. "I'll get us out of this. Somehow."

Just then, the lead guard spotted them. "You there!" he shouted.

Lloyd stepped in front of the princess. "Stay quiet," he whispered.

The guard marched up. "Have you seen anyone hanging around the palace?"

"Hanging around?" Lloyd replied, trying to disguise his voice.

"Yes. Intruders coming or going?"

"Uh, no — I don't think so," Lloyd said.

One of the other guards groaned. "Ugh, this is getting us nowhere," he complained. "The emperor and empress wouldn't have us on patrol if the ninja were just doing their jobs."

I THOUGHT THE NINJA WOULD BE TALLER.

At that, Lloyd frowned. "What do you mean?"

"The ninja are supposed to be protecting the palace," the guard said. "Yet the royal family still has us on patrol."

"I thought the ninja would be taller," a third guard chimed in. "Especially the green one."

Lloyd blushed. But then Princess Harumi poked him. He followed her gaze and spotted an old motorcycle leaning up against the building.

If they could reach it, they could zip away before the guards discovered who they really were.

"What about you?" the lead guard asked Princess Harumi. "Have you seen anything?"

"The ninja seem pretty cool to me," Lloyd interrupted before Princess Harumi could answer. "Which ninja would you be?"

The lead guard laughed. "None of them, thank you very much."

"That ice ninja is kind of cool," another guard said. "I'd be him."

"You mean the *Titanium* Ninja," the third guard corrected him. "And no, *I'd* be him. You can be blue."

"Are you serious?" the other guard replied. "I'm totally the ice ninja. Because I'm cool!"

"Enough of this nonsense," their leader scolded them. "Neither of you are ninja because you are both *royal guards*."

As the guards bickered, Lloyd and Princess Harumi hurried toward the motorcycle. With a zap of green energy, Lloyd got the motor up and running. They sped away without the guards even noticing they were gone.

"Hold tight, Princess!" Lloyd said. "We'll head toward downtown. That way — whoa!"

Suddenly, the front tire blew. Lloyd clung to the handlebars as the motorcycle skidded toward a rail overlooking a cliff!

"Hang on!" cried Princess Harumi. She grabbed the handlebars and pushed Lloyd behind her on the seat. Then the princess revved the engine and leaned into the skid, making the motorcycle turn away from the rail.

With a loud *VROOM*, Lloyd and the princess sped down the street. They zipped up to an alleyway and screeched around a corner.

Lloyd barely had time to catch his breath before the princess shut off the engine. They were safe.

"I — what — *how* did you do that?" he asked in disbelief. "You drove like a master."

"I-I don't know," the princess said. Now that they were stopped, Lloyd could see she was shaking. "I just knew we were in danger — *you* were in danger. And I had to do something. Perhaps it was luck?"

Lloyd was impressed. The more he got to know the princess, the more she amazed him.

"Incredible is what it was." He helped her off the motorcycle. "You saved our lives. Thank you, Princess."

"Do not mention it," Princess Harumi said. "We are lucky to have the ninja protecting the palace."

Lloyd gave a little laugh. "After tonight, I think I should be asking you to protect me."

Princess Harumi smiled shyly. "I will do my best."

GLOSSARY

Airjitzu:
A martial art that allows ninja to leap and fly through the air.

Borg Industries:
The base of Cyrus Borg, an inventor.

communicator:
A tiny device that allows two people to speak from far away.

Cursed Realm:
A dark and gloomy realm where souls are punished for bad deeds.

Elemental Master:
Kai, Nya, and Lloyd are Elemental Masters — ninja with powers over the elements, like fire and water.

monastery:
A home for monks — men of deep faith and religion.

Oni Masks:
Powerful masks that can turn a person evil.

Preeminent:
This monster is the Cursed Realm.

puffy potstickers:
A delicious dumpling served at Master Chen's Noodle Shop.

ransack:
To search and rob.

Sons of Garmadon:
A biker gang who wish to bring back Lord Garmadon in his most evil form.

vengestone:
A grayish-black material that can resist the ninja's elemental powers.

LEGO® BRICK ADVENTURES

ENJOY THESE OTHER
LEGO BRICK ADVENTURES TITLES!